Jungle Adventure

by NORA LOGAN

illustrated by DAVID GOTHARD

SCHOLASTIC INC.

New York Toronto London Auckland Sydney Tokyo

ISBN 0-590-33050-0

Copyright © 1984 by Nora Logan. Illustrations © 1984 by Scholastic, Inc. All rights reserved. Published by Scholastic Inc.

12 11 10 9 8 7 6 5 4 3 2 1   3   4 5 6 7 8/8

Printed in the U.S.A.

To Little Al

—D.G.

Scholastic Books in the Pick-A-Path Series

How many have you read?

READ THIS FIRST

Are you ready for some really fantastic adventures?

Start reading on **page 1** and keep going until you have to make a choice. Then decide what you want to do and turn to that page.

Keep going until you reach **THE END**. Then, you can go back and start again. Every path leads to a new story!

It is all up to you!

You are visiting your Uncle Ned at Jungle Adventure, a wild game park in the Everglades. People drive through the park to look at the birds and animals. There are nature trails for walking, too.

Your uncle runs Jungle Adventure. He's been away all morning and you're feeling a little bored. First you study a large map of the park which is posted next to Ned's house. Maybe when he gets back, you'll go for a hike.

Then you stretch out in a hammock and munch on a granola bar. Through sleepy eyes, you watch a pink flamingo at the edge of a blue lagoon. As a family walks by on the nature trail, the pink bird squawks.

Suddenly you feel a tug on the hammock. WHUMP! You're dumped on the ground.

Turn to **page 2.**

"Hey lazybones, I'm back," says Ned in a cheery voice.

You turn over on your back and smile up at your uncle. He is leading Sweet Pea, his pet elephant, by a long thick rope. Next to your uncle she looks huge!

"Hop on," Ned says.

You've wanted to ride Sweet Pea since you arrived last week. You scramble to your feet and Ned helps you onto the elephant's back.

Then, in the distance, you hear a gunshot.

Uncle Ned frowns. "A hunter must have gotten into the park! I'd better call the sheriff." He drops Sweet Pea's halter and starts for the house.

Just then a second gunshot, much louder than the first, shatters the air. This time Sweet Pea rears up, then crashes through the fence behind the lagoon. Just in time, you grab her halter and hold on for your life.

Turn to **page 4.**

4   You're deep in the forest now and Sweet Pea is still running fast. She runs for miles and miles. Up ahead you see Alligator River. It looks as if Sweet Pea is going to cross it! You know how to swim, but you don't want to meet an alligator in the water. Maybe you should jump off Sweet Pea now, before it's too late.

If you decide to jump off Sweet Pea,
turn to **page 14.**

If you decide to cross the river on
Sweet Pea's back, turn to **page 6.**

Your lungs are bursting and you gulp for air. Then there is silence.

You open your eyes and see that the current has swept you into a cave. The water only comes halfway up the walls of the cave. You can breathe safely now. But if you stay here, no one will ever find you.

You look for a way out and see a tunnel at the back of the cave. You could try to crawl through the tunnel. But you'd hate to get stuck in the middle. You could also rest up and then swim back into the rapids.

If you decide to crawl through the tunnel, turn to **page 47.**

If you decide to swim out of the cave, turn to **page 27.**

6   Sweet Pea plunges into the river. You feel something nip at your foot. You'd better get your feet out of the water! With your legs stretched out behind you, you lie flat on Sweet Pea's back.

You think you're safe. Then the rope slips out of your hand. You're in the water up to your ears!

If you act fast, you might be able to grab Sweet Pea's tail. You could also try swimming back to shore. But you're not sure you can make it in the swift current.

If you try to grab Sweet Pea's tail,
turn to **page 10.**

If you try swimming back to shore,
turn to **page 13.**

"Cut it out!" you laugh. But the water feels great. And you're happy to find Sweet Pea again. Now you can ride her back to the park.

You're so eager to get to her side that you don't look where you're going. At the edge of the swamp you slip on a mossy rock and fall in.

Oh no! The swamp is filled with mud, and you're sinking fast. Already the slimy stuff is up to your waist. You could try to grab the long grass near the edge of the swamp, but you're not sure it will hold you. You could also shout to Sweet Pea who is standing ten feet away. She's trained to come when she hears her name. But if she falls in too, you'll both be lost.

If you try to reach the grass,
turn to **page 56.**

If you call Sweet Pea,
turn to **page 36.**

10   You grab Sweet Pea's tail and she drags you across the river. You are glad to get there in one piece.

You watch Sweet Pea tramp through a tunnel of reeds and decide to follow her. On the other side of the tunnel, she finds a clump of young bamboo and munches on the tender leaves. You see that you are on a strip of land surrounded by a swamp. Three rocks stick out of the water a few feet away.

Wait a minute! The rocks are moving — and they have eyes!

Go on to the next page.

Oh no — alligators! A shiver runs up and down your spine as they open their huge jaws. They start moving toward you.

You have to think fast. You could throw sand at the alligators. Maybe that will give you enough time to reach Sweet Pea. If you can get on her back, you should be safe. But if the sand just makes the alligators angry, you'll be in trouble. Maybe you should simply turn your back and walk away.

If you throw sand at the alligators and run, turn to **page 20.**

If you turn your back and walk away, turn to **page 23.**

You put on your goggles and jump out of the helicopter.

WHOOSH. You whiz through the air very fast. Just in time you remember to pull the cord. The parachute opens and you float gently downward. You are surprised to see that there are dozens of other parachutes all around you.

You land safely and watch the others take off their gear and climb into a truck.

TOP SECRET SPACE TRAINING PROGRAM, says a sign on the truck.

You'll be in big trouble if anyone realizes that you don't belong here.

Turn to **page 39.**

It is hard to swim against the current. But you finally make it to the shore. After you catch your breath you notice an old canoe hidden in the reeds. You also see a dirt track alongside the river.

You remember looking at the map near Ned's house. It shows the Alligator River flowing into the park. You could follow the dirt track by the river, but it might be dark before you make your way back to the park. You would hate to spend the night alone in the forest!

Floating down the river in a canoe would be much faster. But you have a hunch it could also be more dangerous.

What should you do?

If you decide to follow the dirt track,
turn to **page 43.**

If you decide to take the canoe,
turn to **page 52.**

14   You grab a vine and jump off Sweet Pea's back. You swing down to the ground, The light is fading now. Birds chatter and screech. An owl hoots. Twigs snap. All the forest sounds are creepy.

You figure your uncle will follow Sweet Pea's tracks and try to find you. Maybe it would be smart to stay put and wait for him. On the other hand, the trail you followed isn't wide enough for the park jeep. That means your uncle might have to travel on foot. And that could take hours.

If you decide to wait for Ned,
turn to **page 18.**

If you try to get back by yourself,
turn to **page 30.**

16   You turn the canoe around and head for shore. It takes all your strength to paddle against the current. You see two alligators, but they swim away as your canoe bumps against the river bank.

It looks like you'll take the track along the river after all. But first you sit down to rest. About twenty feet away you see a tall palm tree. Underneath, there is a coconut — and it's already cracked open.

Turn to **page 49.**

"Good work," says Ned, ruffling your hair. "This man has been wanted by the police for six months."

"That's right," says the sheriff. He shakes your hand. "I'll make sure the Wildlife Society hears about what you've done. My wife is on the committee."

A week later, all the excitement has died down. You feel a little bored again. After breakfast one morning, Ned has a surprise for you.

"A letter came for you this morning," he says, his eyes twinkling.

For your outstanding bravery, the Wildlife Society invites you to be their guest on a free safari trip to Africa next month.

Yours sincerely,
Humbert Hinkley, President

Wow! Your real jungle adventure hasn't even started. You can't wait for the safari to begin.

THE END

18 You decide to wait. You notice a large tree with a hollow trunk and settle down to wait in front of it. Your eyelids get heavy and you doze for a minute. When you open your eyes you are staring at the face of a large black bear! It is only a few feet away. Too late you realize that the hollow tree is the bear's home.

The bear growls at you, and you run blindly through the woods. You stumble on some branches and fall head over heels into a pit.

Go on to the next page.

Oh no! This must be a trap the hunter set to catch animals —and you've fallen right into it!

A few seconds later, the bear comes crashing down into the pit. Luckily, he doesn't fall on you! And even more luckily, he's a bit stunned from the fall.

You remember that you still have the granola bar in your pocket. Maybe if you give it to the bear, he'll leave you alone. You could also try climbing out of the pit. You don't want to wait for another wild creature to fall into the trap. And you certainly don't want to be here when the hunter returns.

You have to act fast — the bear is beginning to growl.

If you give the granola bar to the bear,
turn to **page 25.**

If you try climbing out of the pit,
turn to **page 22.**

You scoop up some sand and throw it at the alligator closest to you. It stops for a second. But then it comes forward again even faster than before.

Suddenly Sweet Pea lowers her head and charges at the alligator. Raising her huge front hoof, the elephant stomps on its tail. When the other alligators see what has happened, they slink back into the water. A moment later, you feel Sweet Pea's leathery trunk around your waist.

"I'm staying right here with you," you say as she lifts you gently onto her back.

Again and again, Sweet Pea raises her trunk and lets out a strange noise like a trumpet. The cry gets louder and louder until it hurts your ears. But you don't mind at all.

"Now Ned will find us for sure!" you shout, patting the elephant's neck. "Hooray for Sweet Pea!"

THE END

22   You want to get out of the pit. But how can you climb the dirt walls?

Using your shoe, you dig a foothold in the dirt, then manage to climb halfway up. Next you grab onto a tree root that is hanging over the top of the pit. But now the bear is fully awake. You feel its sharp claws dig into your leg. You kick wildly, but this only makes it more angry.

You've got to hold on to the root, or you're finished!

Turn to **page 46.**

You turn around quietly and take two
steps.

SMACK! The alligators' tails thrash in the water. They're coming after you!

You try to run fast, but you trip and fall.

"HELP! HELP!" you shout. But no one can hear you. . . .

Turn to **page 42.**

You toss the granola bar to the bear. While he's busy with the food, you jump on the bear's back and scramble out of the pit.

A few feet from the trap you see a tree covered with vines. The vines give you a great idea. First you find a long one and tie it tight to a sapling. Then you string it over the ground just in front of the trap. With one end of the vine in your hand, you hide behind a tree.

Turn to **page 26.**

26 You wait a long time. Then you hear footsteps. The hunter is coming to see what has fallen into his trap. When he reaches the right spot, you pull the vine tight and trip him.

Turn to **page 44.**

You take a deep breath and swim out of the cave. Just when you think the end has come, the swirling water carries you into a calm lagoon.

You take a great gulp of air and look around.

You made it! You're in the middle of the blue lagoon. Pink flamingos squawk as you wade out of the pond. You're exhausted from your adventure and decide to rest in the hammock until your uncle gets back.

Next time you'll think twice before riding Sweet Pea. You had no idea that elephant rides could be so dangerous!

THE END

You struggle to turn around and look up. Your parachute is caught on the tusks of a giant elephant! Every ten seconds, the fake animal raises and lowers its head, swinging you up and down.

"WILL SOMEBODY TURN OFF THE ELEPHANT?" you shout. But everyone is busy watching the fireworks.

You keep shouting for a while. Then you give up.

You've been tossed in the rapids, lost in a cave, and trapped in a runaway helicopter. And after all that, you're stuck in the jungle with another elephant! What a way for this adventure to come to

THE END

You find Sweet Pea's tracks in the soft ground and follow her trail. But soon it's too dark to see very well. You find a soft bed of ferns and go to sleep.

In the morning you feel something cold and slithery on your chest. It slides slowly over your body. You open one eye.

Go on to the next page.

A large yellow snake is curled up on your leg! Its head is raised, ready to strike. Your blood turns cold and you try not to move.

"Hold your breath!" a voice says. And a second later, your uncle grabs the snake and flings it away.

"Just in time!" you say to your uncle as he gives you a big hug.

Turn to **page 32.**

Walking back to the house with Ned, you keep feeling the snake on your leg. You still feel scared.

"What happened?" your uncle asks. "I was worried when Sweet Pea came home alone last night."

You tell him about jumping off the elephant just before the Alligator River.

"Imagine that," Ned says. "I was going to take you to the river myself. But Sweet Pea beat me to it," he laughs. "We could still go canoeing tomorrow and look for alligators."

You're not ready for another jungle adventure. One runaway elephant and one poisonous snake are more than enough.

"No thanks, Uncle Ned. I'll stay near the house for a while. And next vacation, I think I'll go skiing."

THE END

You climb into the helicopter to wait for them. As you sit down, you bump into a lever. Suddenly the motor roars. In panic, you pull on a knob, hoping to turn off the motor. Instead the big blades whirl overhead and the helicopter takes off!

You watch the trees and rivers shrink to dots and ribbons as you go higher.

The machine is flying steadily now and you begin to enjoy the ride.

You notice a parachute pack on the pilot's seat and put it on just in case.

"Sput . . . sput . . . clang . . ." The control dials are going crazy. Then the engine stops.

If you try to start the engine,
turn to **page 54.**

If you jump out and hope that
the parachute works,
turn to **page 12.**

The canoe enters the rapids. Desperately you try to keep the boat pointing forward. But the swirling water is too powerful. White spray is all around you. And the roar of the water is like thunder.

CRACK! The canoe smashes into the rocks and you are tossed overboard. Again and again, the churning waves pull you under the water.

Turn to **page 5.**

"Sweet Pea! Sweet Pea!" you shout.

When she hears her name, the elephant flaps her huge ears. Then she walks carefully to the edge of the swamp. Her front legs sink a few inches in the muck and she backs off. Cautiously, she kneels down and extends her trunk. You can reach it!

Turn to **page 38.**

38　　You hold on tight to the elephant's trunk. Inch by inch, Sweet Pea backs up. Your arms feel like they are going to fall off. But finally, she drags you out of the mud, then lifts you onto her back.

Sweet Pea finds the track near the river and starts walking. Soon you pass a quiet spot and catch a glimpse of yourself in the calm water.

Eeeeeeeeek. What a sight! Covered with mud from head to toe, you look really weird.

You feel the mud on your face crack as you start to smile. If the hunter is watching, he'll be frightened away for good!

THE END

Nobody sees you as you get into the truck. "Just think," says the woman beside you to her friend. "Next week we'll be on a secret mission to Jupiter!"

After the truck pulls up beside a low building, you follow the others inside. First everyone puts on a spacesuit. Then one by one they enter a clear plastic tunnel. Your turn comes. At the end of the passage, you find yourself floating upside down in a bubble-shaped room.

You are weightless. You are having so much fun that you decide to keep quiet about the mistake.

Come to think of it, you wouldn't mind being an astronaut. By this time next week, you might even be on your way to Jupiter!

THE END

You walk over to the palm tree and pick up the coconut. As you take a bite of the delicious white coconut, a net falls over your head.

The hunter steps out from behind a tree. "What's this?" he says, scratching his head. "I was after a bear and I got a kid!"

You beg him to let you go, but he won't listen. He thinks you will run to the police. So he throws you into a cage in the back of his van.

The next day he drops you off at a traveling circus.

You like the circus people and they like you. You become an acrobat. High above the crowds, you walk on a tight-rope and swing on a trapeze.

You miss your family, but circus life is exciting — and you don't have to go to school. Maybe someday you'll go home, but for now you are happy being the star of the show!

THE END

"Wake up! Wake up!" says a voice. "You're having a bad dream."

You still feel scared when you open your eyes. But the alligators fade away. You sit up and look around. You're still in the hammock near the blue lagoon. Ned is looking down at you.

"Feeling better?" he asks. "The heat will give you nightmares every time."

You smile uncertainly. You still feel a little shaky.

"I have an idea," Ned says. "Something to chase all the ghosts and goblins away. How would you like to go for a ride on Sweet Pea?"

Oh no! Not again!

THE END

You take the dirt track along the river. After a few miles you stop for a rest.

Out of nowhere a stream of water gushes over your sweaty face. You whirl around and see Sweet Pea grazing calmly near the edge of a swamp. She sucks the water up through her trunk, then sprays you again.

Turn to **page 9.**

"YEOOW," the hunter yells, tumbling down into the pit. When he hits the bottom, he yells even louder and grabs hold of his ankle. He sees the snarling bear, and his face turns white.

Whoopee! Your plan worked. With his injured ankle and that bear watching him, the hunter is trapped.

A few minutes later, Ned and the sheriff run into the clearing. They see the hunter and their mouths drop open in surprise.

Turn to **page 17.**

You think fast. You could try paddling
ashore. But if the boat sinks, the alligators will probably get you. Maybe you
should try going over the rapids. It will
be rough going, but at least you won't
be eaten alive!

If you try paddling ashore,
turn to **page 16.**

If you try going over the rapids,
turn to **page 35.**

46　　"I can do it . . . I can do it . . . I can do it . . ." you say to yourself.

But your hand is sweaty now. And the root slips through your fingers. You close your eyes tight as you tumble back into the pit. . . .

Turn to **page 50.**

You crawl through the tunnel. The icy water is up to your neck. But finally you see sunlight. When you crawl outside, you see a helicopter on the ground next to a palm tree. It is empty.

You walk closer and see STATE POLICE printed on its side.

All your worries are over. Ned must have called the sheriff to help him search for you. They are sure to be close by.

Turn to **page 33.**

At the sight of food, your stomach growls. You're really hungry. Then you remember the hunter and you feel a jolt of fear. What if the hunter is hiding among the palm trees?

If you stay and eat the coconut, turn to **page 40.**

If you take the dirt track, turn to **page 43.**

50 The next day you wake up in bed with a bandaged leg. Ned is smiling down at you.

"How did you find me?" you ask. "Did you catch the hunter?"

Ned touches your lips with his finger. "There will be plenty of time for questions later on. The doctor says you have to sleep now."

You want to talk to him about your adventure . . . about Sweet Pea, and the bear, and the hunter, and . . . before you can open your mouth again, you fall fast asleep.

THE END

You push the canoe into the river. There is a paddle inside. The current sweeps you downstream. You try to relax and enjoy the ride. But you see alligators along the shore. Their sharp teeth gleam in the sunlight. They look mean.

As you go around a bend, you see rapids ahead. The crashing, swirling water roars in your ears. At the same time you realize that your feet are wet. The canoe is leaking!

Turn to **page 45.**

54　　How can you start the engine? Desperately you look at the control panel. You push a button marked "RESERVE FUEL" and the engine starts humming again.

You relax for a while and fly west into the sunset. As a flaming red sun sinks below the horizon, the fuel gauge hits EMPTY.

You'd better figure out how to land — and fast!

Suddenly the sky explodes with gold and silver sparkles. Crowds of people fill the streets below. Looking down, you can't believe your eyes.

Go on to the next page.

Snow White and the Seven Dwarfs are leading a parade. Another burst of fireworks lights up a fairy-tale castle.

Of course. You're flying over Disney World!

You see a sign that says JUNGLE RIVER RIDE. Nearby there is an island with a beach. You try to land there, away from the crowd. But the tail of the helicopter hits a tall palm tree.

The crash throws you out of the helicopter. You close your eyes, waiting to smash into the ground. But you stop suddenly a few feet above the beach.

Turn to **page 28.**

You struggle toward the edge of the swamp. Yuck! The mud is almost up to your neck. With great effort, you twist some long grass in both hands and pull.

Nothing happens. You pull harder, and the grass snaps off in your hand.

Better luck next time!

Glurp . . . glurp . . . glurp . . .

THE END